Downtown Lost and Found

Written by Frank B. Edwards
Illustrated by John Bianchi

gate

bird

key   lock

rhinoceros

bear

elephant

tiger

lion

giraffe

ostrich

Downtown

snake

monkey

I am lost.

Wait in here and you will be found.

We are lost.

Wait in here and you will be found.

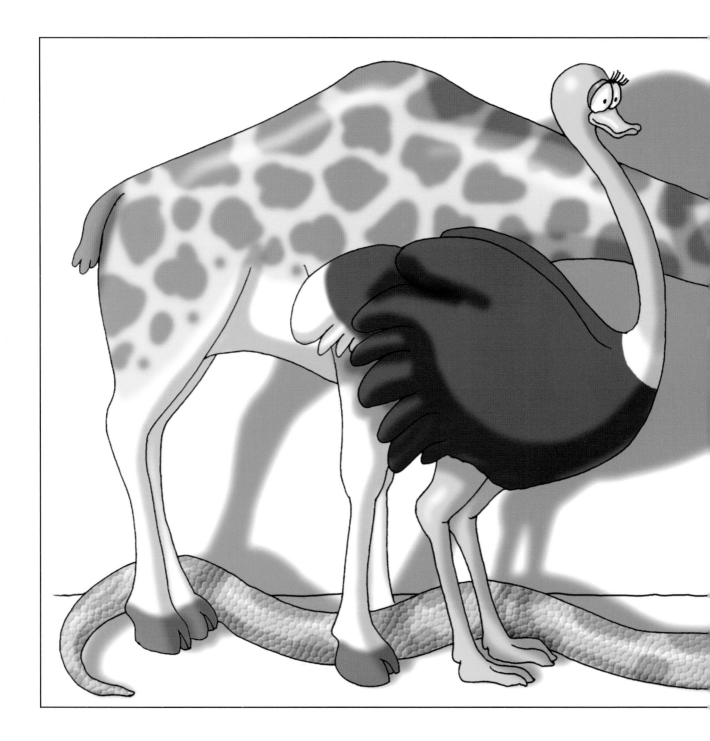

We are lost.

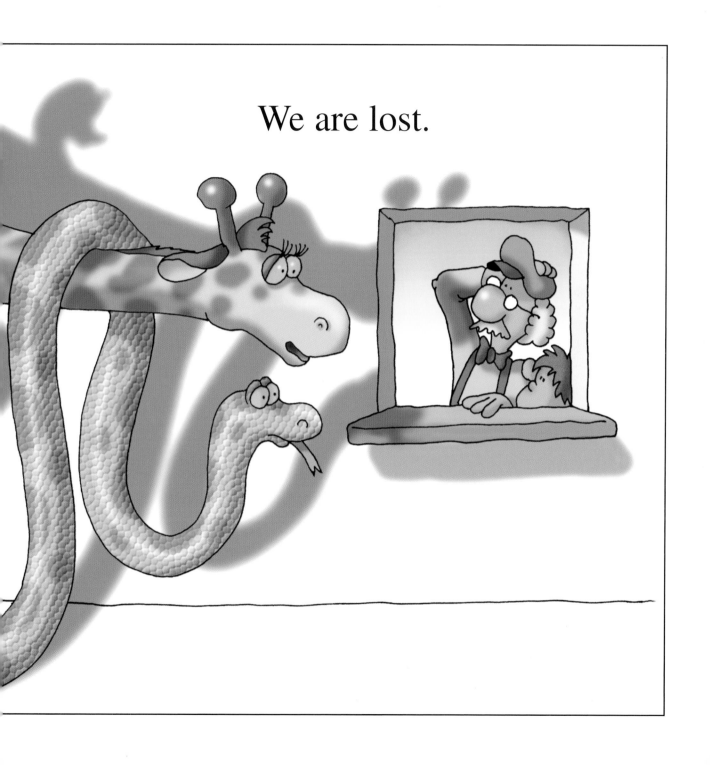

Wait in here and you will be found.

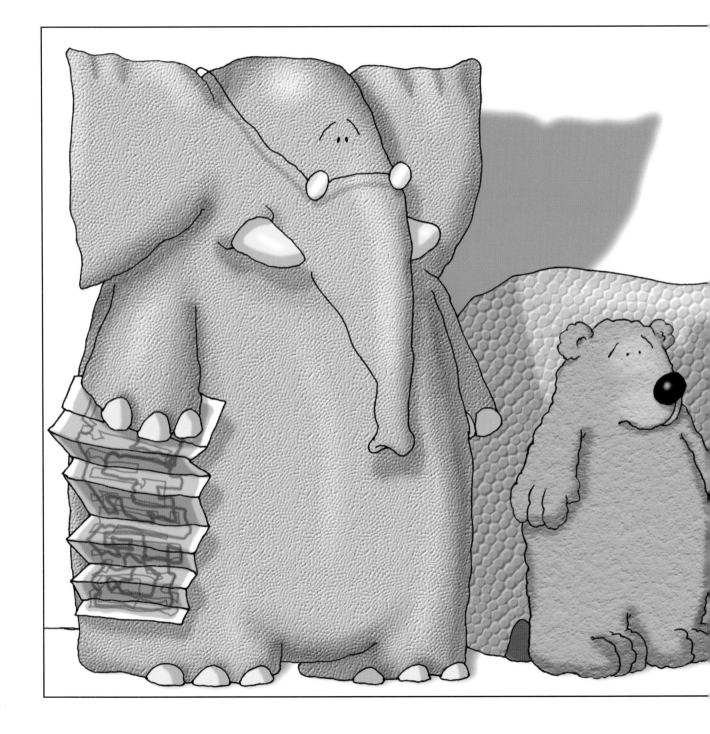

We are lost.

Wait in here and
you will be found.

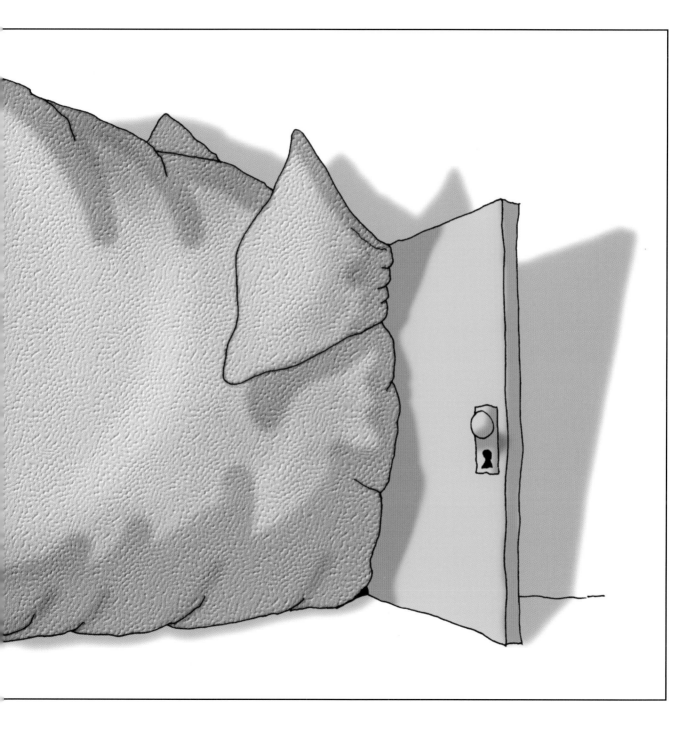

My animals are lost.

Look in here.

The End